For Frances Foster and

in memory of Christopher Ray, a great artist

HOKUSAI

THE MAN WHO PAINTED A MOUNTAIN

Deborah Kogan Ray

FRANCES FOSTER BOOKS

FARRAR, STRAUS AND GIROUX

NEW YORK

Long ago in Japan, there was a man who made more than thirty thousand works of art. We know him as Hokusai, which means "north star studio." It is one of more than thirty names that he used as an artist. Each name reflected a change in his life and his art. We call him Hokusai because his most famous work of art, and one of the world's great masterpieces, *Thirty-six Views of Mount Fuji,* is signed that way.

He called himself the peasant from Katsushika.

Low-lying and marshy, Katsushika district was home to the poorest people of the great and growing city of Edo, now known as Tokyo. It is where Hokusai was born in 1760, in the Honjo quarter beside the Wari-gesi canal. His mother called him Tokitaro, "firstborn son." He had no family name; his father is unknown.

Tokitaro 辰太郎

"From the age of five, I needed to sketch the form of things."

Mount Fuji 富士山

Across the Sumida River, the shogun and his samurai soldiers lived in splendor high on a hill. But the sun rarely shone on the shops and houses of the people of the Honjo quarter. On days when the fog lifted from the swampy land, the boy could see glints of snow, above the shogun's castle, outlining the peak of Mount Fuji.

To the boy, the mountain was magic.

From the time he had been a baby, his mother sang to him about the sun goddess who smiled on them from Fuji, Japan's most sacred mountain.

Though now too sick to move from her mat, his mother promised that they would make a pilgrimage in the spring. She said cherry trees bloomed, like billowing clouds, on the path that they would follow. With a bamboo stick, the boy drew the mountain's shape in the courtyard dirt and imagined what they would see.

"I will make many pictures," he promised.

But Hokusai never walked among the cherry blossoms with his mother. She died when he was six years old.

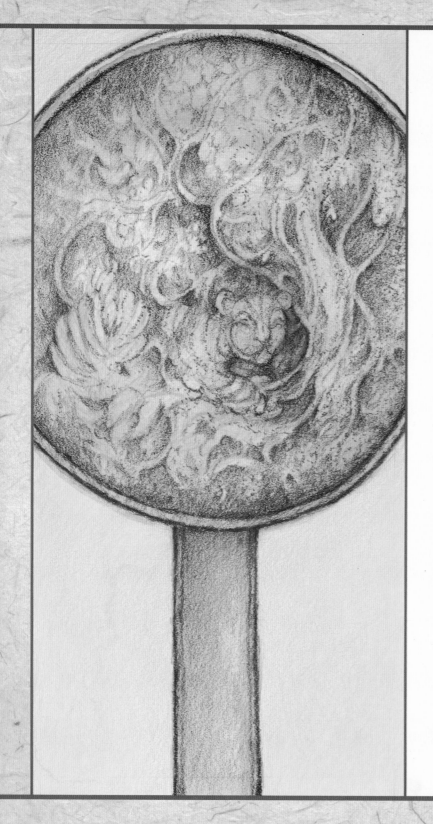

Hokusai's Uncle Ise took him to live with his family and work in his shop, polishing mirrors for the shogun's court. But the boy did not feel welcome in the Nakajima home. His uncle sternly warned Hokusai that he would be punished if he did not work hard and obey all the rules.

In those days, Japanese mirrors were not made of glass. The backs and handles were cast in bronze, with a silvered surface for the face. The shop was always busy because the faces tarnished quickly and needed to be polished often.

Hour after hour, Hokusai's reflection stared at him as he rubbed the mirror faces. As hard as he tried to obey and to concentrate only on his task, his thoughts wandered to the decorations on the mirror backs. Many told stories from ancient legends. His fingers traced the horses and tigers, birds, trees, and twining vines. He wanted to hear the stories. He wanted to draw them.

Often, Hokusai felt the sting of his uncle's bamboo switch when he left a scratch on the mirror because he was not paying attention to his polishing.

He was different from his cousins. They laughed at his interest in the pictures on the mirror backs. After finishing their polishing, they ran out to the street for games. Hokusai stayed behind in the shop. When he was certain he was alone, he drew on scraps of wrapping paper, using charcoal from the stove.

"I had a passion for drawing."

Mirror shop 鏡屋

When Hokusai was a boy, a succession of shoguns had reigned over Japan for more than one hundred and fifty years.

While the emperor lived in secluded majesty in the imperial city of Kyoto, the shogun ruled the country from the city of Edo. It was a military government. The word *shogun* means "general." He gave orders, and his powerful samurai soldiers enforced his commands. There were strict rules for the people. They were told how to dress and what they were allowed to eat, according to their rank. To be obedient and never to question Japanese customs were the most important rules. Long before Hokusai was born, all foreigners had been banished. Exchange of goods was made with Dutch traders on a distant island, but they were not allowed to enter or live in Japan because the shogun did not want ideas from the outside world to reach the people.

Though the shogun controlled what the people were taught, education was considered very important. The children of artisans, like Uncle Ise, were taught by Buddhist priests in small temple schools called *tera-koya*.

Hokusai welcomed the afternoons that he was sent for lessons with the priests. While his cousins dawdled on their way, he rushed down the street to the temple, took his seat on the floor, and eagerly waited for class to begin. He loved the feel of the ink-dipped brush in his hand as he formed the shapes of the writing, called kanji, that had come to Japan from China. The Chinese characters looked like the things they represented. Each word looked like a picture.

鳥
Bird

木
Tree

葉
Leaf

虎
Tiger

花
Flower

馬
Horse

竹
Bamboo

"I set my heart on learning."

Bookshop 本屋

When Hokusai was twelve years old and his schooling had ended, he discovered a lending library from which books were borrowed for a fee. He could not believe so many books existed.

Shelves were filled with novels about famous warriors and tales of ancient times. Tables were piled with colorful picture books. Opening one after another, he stared in wonder at the beautiful illustrations. He wished he could borrow all of the books, but he could not afford the fee for even one.

At night, he dreamed about the books. Day after day, when his work in his uncle's shop was done, he ran to the lending library and stayed until it closed. Gathering all his courage, he persuaded the owner to let him live in the shop and study from the books.

"I need only a bowl of noodle soup for dinner and I will do any work you ask," Hokusai said.

All day, he carried a heavy pack loaded with books for borrowing through the busy streets of Edo. He tended the shop and swept the floor. When his work was done, he read and drew. With his heart set on learning, he copied illustrations made by famous artists.

After three years, he was able to imitate many styles of painting. One customer was so impressed by Hokusai's copies that he offered him an apprenticeship as a woodblock engraver in his printing shop.

Engravers made the book illustrations from paintings by the artists that Hokusai admired. He was eager to begin his new life.

The printing shop was a busy place. Three people worked on each picture.

The artist, called the *eshi*, designed the picture and made a black outline drawing of it on thin rice paper. This was called a draft.

The engraver, the *hori-shi*, glued the draft onto a block of hard cherry wood, then, using a mallet and sharp tools, carved the picture into the woodblock. Great skill and delicate technique were needed in carving. The success or failure of a print depended on how well it was cut.

The printer, the *suri-shi*, inked colored pigments into the grooves carved by the engraver. Long-fibered paper was laid on top of the woodblock, then rubbed with a round bamboo pressing pad called a *baren* to transfer the inked picture to the paper from the woodblock. When the artist decided that the engraving and colors were correct, the *suri-shi* printed the edition. Many copies could be made by working this way.

In Hokusai's hands, chisels and knives captured each brushstroke of the artist's picture. He became so skilled as a woodblock engraver that many artists asked to work with him. The great master Shunsho refused to work with any other engraver in the shop.

Printshop 印刷屋　　Artist 絵師　　Engraver 彫り師　　Printer 刷り師

When Hokusai was eighteen years old, Shunsho invited him to become his pupil. It was a great honor to be the student of a famous master. To Hokusai, it was a dream come true.

"Now I shall become an artist," he said.

Shunsho was an ukiyo-e artist. He made pictures of the "floating world." To the people of Edo, the "floating world" embraced the things they regarded as pleasures. Kabuki theater actors, sumo wrestlers, dancers, and beautiful women were the subjects of Shunsho's paintings and prints. He drew with an elegant line and painted graceful shapes.

Shunsho's students learned to paint the way he did. Hokusai made prints, posters, and books that looked like Shunsho's work. He took the name Shunro, in honor of his master and to celebrate his new life as an artist of the "floating world."

Soon he was selling his own pictures to the wealthy merchants who were the patrons of Shunsho's studio. He saved enough money to marry.

春
朗
画

Shunro signature

Ukiyo-e 浮世絵

In the "floating world" of the city of Edo, carefree crowds filled the streets, the tea-houses, and the theaters. Hokusai joined them at Kabuki plays. He knew many of the actors because they came to Shunsho's studio to pose for paintings. They were all men, even those who played women's roles. Hokusai painted the great Danjuro V, who was famous for playing superheroes.

The nobility of Japan attended the serious Noh dramas. Kabuki was the theater of the ordinary people. Performances lasted all day and had music, dance, and lots of action. The actors wore elaborate costumes. Heroes swaggered and brandished swords. Audiences knew the plots of most of the plays because the stories came from old legends and tales. The spectators ate, drank, and gossiped in the aisles that surrounded the stage. At exciting moments in the play, they stopped their conversations and cheered. Kabuki fans loved it when the leading actor struck and held a dramatic pose called a *mie*. The actor shook his head in rhythm to a loud drumbeat, then crossed his eyes in a fierce glare for the final touch to a special *mie*.

The Kabuki actor Danjuro V was a favorite subject of the artists of the "floating world."   Kabuki 歌舞伎

"I was firmly established."

Festival 祭

The center of Edo became a huge carnival during holiday festivals. People filled the streets and strolled on the Ryogoku Bridge. They ate broiled eel, sushi, and other delicacies bought from carts. They watched puppet shows and performing monkeys. Musicians played. Poets recited. Quick-draw sword artists and basket jumpers entertained the crowds. Fireworks lit the sky.

As a boy, Hokusai had been too poor to attend these festivals. He would not have been welcome among people of higher social rank. Now, drawing in his sketchbook, he mingled comfortably with the crowds. He loved the color and the movement of the sea of people. Sometimes he climbed onto rooftops to get a better view.

Shunsho was still his master, but Hokusai was no longer a student. He was a recognized artist with his own studio and patrons. Publishers of books and posters kept him working from morning to night filling orders for pictures of the most popular subjects of the "floating world." It was expected that Hokusai would become the master and have many pupils when the aging Shunsho died.

For a young man who had been so poor, it was a very exciting life.

When the shogun allowed the Dutch traders to bring books and prints by artists from faraway Europe to Japan, Hokusai was excited by how real the pictures looked. He filled the walls of his studio with them and copied the style of the European artists, using shading and perspective. His paintings did not look flat like ukiyo-e pictures; things close up were big, things far away appeared small. He called them "Landscapes in the Western Way."

His publishers told him that no one would want to see his pictures in books because they did not look Japanese. Hokusai did not care.

He studied the works of ancient Chinese artists and painted flowers, birds, and tree branches in the delicate manner that they did. He called himself Sori, after a Japanese master who painted in the Chinese style.

The art world of Japan had many rules. Artists who painted like Shunsho were angered by all of Hokusai's new pictures. They told him that he held his head too high and thought only of himself. He was warned that an artist must be faithful to one master.

"There are many other ways of painting that I must learn," Hokusai told them.

Sori signature

Often Hokusai wandered through the working districts of Edo with his sketchbook. At the docks, he drew fishermen. In the marketplace, he drew the vendors and farmers loading carts.

This was the world that Hokusai had known since childhood. Its bustling crowds, smells, and sounds were familiar to him. He joked with the people he drew. His sketches were lively. Many of them were funny. He made hundreds and hundreds of drawings.

"I am a peasant from Katsushika," Hokusai replied to those who ridiculed his drawings for their lack of elegance and called them unrefined.

"I must paint the way my heart tells me," he told his wealthy patrons when they refused to buy his pictures of laboring artisans and humble farmers toiling in fields.

He was happy to be free of the rules dictated by a master, but independence had a heavy price. With fewer patrons, Hokusai could not earn a living. To feed his wife and three children, he peddled red peppers and calendars while he walked the streets of Edo with his sketchbook.

Hokusai's sketchbooks, his *Manga*, contain hundreds of pictures of people at work.   *Manga* 漫画

"I knew the will of heaven and was ready to listen to it."

Light spring rain fell on the pilgrims who crowded the path that led to the temple on Mount Fuji.

Hokusai walked slowly. His heart was heavy. He had said his prayers of remembrance for his wife, who had died. Sadness filled him with memories. He thought of his mother and the courtyard of their house. The sacred mountain had appeared magical to him when he saw it through the clouds.

"When I was a small boy, I promised that I would make many pictures of this mountain," he told his children.

At the age of thirty-six, Hokusai took the name we call him.

To Hokusai, "north star studio" was a place of the heart. As a Buddhist, he believed in the power of heaven's constellations to guide him. He looked to the star that shone most constantly, ever unreachable, but always there.

Hokusai signature

The sacred mountain became part of Hokusai's life. He observed it from every distance and angle. He drew it in all seasons, at every time of day. He painted its flowers, birds, and trees. He painted it with people working and playing. He painted it touched by gentle mist and surrounded by roaring seas. He painted its peak in every mood and weather.

Over many, many years, he drew and painted the mountain again and again.

Hokusai's masterpiece, *Thirty-six Views of Mount Fuji*, was completed when he was over seventy years old. In these colored woodblock prints are all the things that Hokusai had learned and all the wonder that he felt.

"I followed my heart's desire."

This woodcut by Hokusai is from *Thirty-six Views of Mount Fuji*. He called it "The Great Wave off Kanagawa."

Late in Hokusai's life, scholars asked Japan's famous master to sum up his work as an artist.

"From the age of five," Hokusai wrote to them, "I have needed to sketch the form of things. Yet of all I drew prior to the age of seventy, there is truly nothing of great note.

"At the age of seventy-two, I finally understood something of the quality of birds, animals, insects, fish, and the nature of grass and trees. Therefore at eighty, I shall have made some progress. At ninety, I shall have penetrated even further the meaning of things. At one hundred, I shall have become truly marvelous, and at one hundred and ten, each dot and every line will surely possess a life of its own."

Though crippled and bent, Hokusai still rose early and continued painting until well after dark.

The name he called himself was Gakyo Rojin, "old man mad about painting."

Gakyo Rojin signature

Every morning Hokusai sketched a lion-dog drawing to bring him good luck.

KATSUSHIKA HOKUSAI (1760–1849)

The artist we know as Hokusai lived a remarkable life. By numbers alone, his productivity of thirty thousand works of art is amazing.

He made thousands of drawings, woodblock prints, copper plate engravings, book illustrations, posters, albums, fans, paintings on paper and silk, large screens, and miniatures. It is said that once he painted a picture of sparrows on a grain of rice.

He delighted in displays of his artistic skill and made gigantic paintings of mythological figures in front of admiring audiences.

He painted landscapes, portraits, theater pictures, animals, fish, and birds. He drew thousands of figure sketches of people and made illustrations for warrior tales and ghost stories.

His fifteen volumes of the *Hokusai Manga*, published as how-to-draw books, cover an amazing range of subjects—everything from comb and pipe designs to drawings of mice and dragons, fishermen, barrel makers, noodle makers, and fat and thin people.

As a person, he was strong-willed and restless. He changed his place of residence more than ninety times. He cared nothing about money and was a terrible businessman. Despite his fame, he remained poor all his life. His life revolved around his art.

To have emerged from the peasant class in Japan, at the time he lived, was something rare. To have become a great artist of his country was astonishing.

Not only did Hokusai change the art of Japan, he changed art in the Western world. The famous French Impressionists and Post-Impressionists of the last century were all influenced by him. Edouard Manet, Edgar Degas, Mary Cassatt, Paul Gauguin, and Vincent van Gogh would not have painted in the way they did if not for Hokusai.

Hokusai died in his ninetieth year. Crowds followed his plain coffin to a temple in Asakura, not far from where he was born. Leading the procession were one hundred of the shogun's samurai.

Even as a ghost
I'll gaily tread
the summer moors.

Hokusai's parting haiku
inscribed on his
gravestone

CHRONOLOGY

1603 Rule of Tokugawa shoguns begins. Edo becomes capital of Japan.

1639 Shogun establishes policy of national seclusion; foreigners are banished.

1760 Hokusai is born in Edo.

1775 Begins apprenticeship as woodblock engraver.

1778 Enters the studio of Katsukawa Shunsho.

1779 Issues his first prints as Shunro.

1795 Adopts the name Sori.

1796 First uses the name Hokusai.

1799 Announces his name change to Hokusai. He adopts other names frequently throughout his art career, but retains Hokusai as his official name.

1814 First volume of *Hokusai Manga* published.

1830–35 *Thirty-six Views of Mount Fuji* published.

1834–35 *One Hundred Views of Mount Fuji* published.

1849 Hokusai dies.

1854 Treaty of Kanagawa opens trade between Japan and the United States.

1856 In France, Impressionist etching artist Félix Bracquemond finds a volume of the *Hokusai Manga* used as packing in a box of imported ceramics.

1868 Tokugawa shogun overthrown. Emperor Meiji establishes imperial rule and opens Japan to all the world.

Illustrations executed in watercolor and colored pencil on D'Arche 140-pound hot-press watercolor paper

The Great Wave off Kanagawa: courtesy of The Metropolitan Museum of Art, H. O. Havemeyer Collection, Bequest of Mrs. H. O. Havemeyer, 1929. (JP 1847) Photograph © 1994 The Metropolitan Museum of Art

Endpapers: Drawings from the *Hokusai Manga,* volumes I, II, III, IV, VIII

SELECTED BIBLIOGRAPHY

Forrer, Matthi. *Hokusai: Prints and Drawings*. Prestel-Verlag, 1991.

Hillier, J. *Hokusai Drawings*. Phaidon, 1966.

Ives, Colta Feller. *The Great Wave: The Influence of Japanese Woodcuts on French Prints*. The Metropolitan Museum of Art, 1974.

Lane, Richard. *Hokusai: Life and Work*. E. P. Dutton, 1989.

Lane, Richard. *Images from the Floating World*. Chartwell Books, 1978.

Michener, James. *The Hokusai Sketchbooks: Selections from the Manga*. Charles E. Tuttle, 1958.

Nagata, Seiji. *Hokusai: Genius of the Japanese Ukiyo-e*. Trans. John Bester. Kodansha International, 1995.

Narazaki, Muneshige. *Hokusai: Sketches and Paintings*. Kodansha International, 1969.

Nishiyama, Matsunosuke. *Edo Culture: Daily Life and Diversions in Urban Japan, 1600–1868*. Trans. Gerald Gromer. University of Hawaii Press, 1997.

Ripley, Elizabeth. *Hokusai: A Biography*. J. B. Lippincott, 1968.

Copyright © 2001 by Deborah Kogan Ray
All rights reserved
Distributed in Canada by Douglas & McIntyre Ltd.
Color separations by Hong Kong Scanner Arts
Printed and bound in the United States of America
by Berryville Graphics
Designed by Filomena Tuosto
Kanji and translations by Megumi Suzuki McKeever of the
Japan-America Society of Philadelphia
First edition, 2001
1 3 5 7 9 10 8 6 4 2

Library of Congress Cataloging-in-Publication Data
Ray, Deborah Kogan, date.
    Hokusai : the man who painted a mountain / Deborah Kogan Ray.
        p.   cm.
    ISBN 0-374-33263-0
    1. Katsushika, Hokusai, 1760–1849—Juvenile literature.
    2. Printmakers—Japan—Biography—Juvenile literature.
    [1. Katsushika, Hokusai, 1760–1849. 2. Artists. 3. Art, Japanese.]
    I. Title.

NE1325.K3 R39 2001
769.92—dc21

00-50395